THE Berenstain BEAR SCOUTS

Scream Their Heads Off

THE Berenstain BEAR SCOUTS
Scream Their Heads Off

by Stan & Jan Berenstain
Illustrated by Michael Berenstain

A
LITTLE APPLE
PAPERBACK

SCHOLASTIC INC.
New York Toronto London Auckland Sydney

ISBN 0-590-94484-3

Copyright © 1998 by Berenstain Enterprises, Inc.
All rights reserved. Published by Scholastic Inc.
LITTLE APPLE PAPERBACKS and associated logos
are trademarks of Scholastic Inc.

12 11 10 9 8 7 6 5 4 3 2 1   8 9/9 0 1 2 3/0

Printed in the U.S.A.   40

First Scholastic printing, June 1998

• Contents •

Scream Their
Heads Off

• Chapter 1 •
The House on the Hill

When folks drove out of Beartown they usually took the main road that went to Big Bear City. But although the road went to the city, folks didn't always follow it all the way there. Often they went only as far as Bear Country Mall to shop, or Birder's Woods for a nature hike, or Two-Ton Grizzly's auto graveyard to buy auto parts.

On the way back, the main road ran through the middle of town, where it was called Main Street, and kept right on going out the other side, away from both Beartown and Big Bear City. But no one

1

ever seemed to drive out that way. That's because out there, beyond Beartown's city limits, the main road hadn't been kept up for years and years. It was easy to bust a wheel or break an axle in one of those yawning cracks or gaping potholes. At least, that's what most Beartown folks said.

But if you asked one of Beartown's older folks — Grizzly Gramps, for instance — about that stretch of road, he'd just smile and say, "Oh, it ain't that bad."

You'd say, "But I heard nobody ever goes out that way because it hasn't been kept up."

To which Gramps would answer, "You heard it backwards, friend. That road hasn't been kept up because nobody ever goes out there."

"I guess that's not surprising," you'd say. "Folks tell me there's nothing out that way worth visiting."

At that, Gramps would give a little chuckle and say, "They've got that sort of backwards, too. What they mean is, there's *something* out that way that's worth *stayin' away from*."

That something was a place called Spook Hill. It was a few miles out of town, near the spot where the main road just sort of petered out. From the road's dead end, a narrow dirt path angled up the hillside, ran through the gate in the broken-down iron fence that surrounded the hilltop, and came to rest at a house. A very old, empty, lonesome-looking house, sitting all by itself on the top of Spook Hill.

It wasn't called the old Bruin house, or the old Grizzly house, or the McGrizz house, or some such thing after the name of an owner or former owner. Most folks simply called it the House on Spook Hill. In fact, most folks didn't even know who owned it.

Who owned the old house on Spook Hill wasn't the only thing about it that was mysterious. There were plenty of questions whose answers folks wondered about. For instance, what did the old house look like inside? Too-Tall Grizzly and his gang were the only ones in town, cub or grown-up, who claimed to have been inside it, or even to have seen it up close. One summer day, when twilight was settling over the countryside, they had climbed Spook Hill on a dare — or so they said — and come back to town with a wild story. A story about a neglected path so overgrown with thorny underbrush that their clothes were ripped to shreds and their fur had to be clipped to get the burs out. About a musty old house full of cobwebs and snaggle-toothed broken windows and rotting, fall-through floors and scurrying rats with glowing yellow eyes. About an ancient belfry that spat black

clouds of bats the way a squid squirts ink. And about a little graveyard that lay next to the house — not an *auto* graveyard, mind you, but a *real* one — of crumbling tombstones tangled in creepers and thornbushes, where weird, shadowy forms appeared in the dusk and moaned and wailed.

Cubs didn't know, of course, whether Too-Tall and his gang were telling the truth or not. They might have been exaggerating, or even just plain lying, to impress everyone with their courage. But their story did square with what old Josiah Bruin had once told his grandcubs: Spook Hill was haunted by ghosts from a graveyard there. And that wasn't the only rumor about ghosts on Spook Hill. According to Farmer Ben, the old house itself was haunted, too, by the ghosts of a murdered family that had once lived there.

Cubs didn't know whether to believe one rumor or the other, or both, or neither. Usually grown-ups weren't much help when asked about the House on Spook Hill. Most just said it was a dangerous place that cubs should stay away from. And others wouldn't even answer — just get very quiet for a moment, with a nervous look in their eyes, then change the subject.

There was something about Spook Hill that did seem certain, though. It was a place lost in time, fast asleep in a distant past that would remain forever shrouded in mystery. No new chapters in its haunted history would ever be written. Except, perhaps, for one final chapter written by a wrecking ball.

But histories have a funny way of taking unexpected twists and turns. And that was true of Spook Hill's history. One lazy Beartown summer, a new Spook Hill chapter *was* written. Not by a wrecking ball, but by our friends the Bear Scouts.

• Chapter 2 •
An Urgent Meeting

The sounds of cubs arguing in the Bear Scouts' secret clubhouse were getting so loud that they might well have disturbed the neighbors if the scouts had had any neighbors to disturb. Luckily, the clubhouse was in an old chicken coop on the far side of Farmer Ben's farm, where the only creatures that could be disturbed were the chickens that occasionally dropped by to visit their former home.

"No!" cried Scout Brother, pounding the little table he always sat behind to lead

scout meetings. "Not the *Basket-weaving* Merit Badge! Anything but that!"

The scouts were trying to decide which merit badge to go for next. The problem was that they already had all the good ones. The badges they had earned in the past were all tacked to a ribbon that hung on the Honor Wall next to a framed copy of the Bear Scout Oath. They included, among others, the Wilderness Survival Merit Badge, the Water Safety Merit Badge, the Good Deed Merit Badge, and the History Merit Badge.

Scout Lizzy made a mopey face at Brother. She didn't like being yelled at. "Well, then," she said, "what about the Banjo Band Merit Badge?"

Brother stared at Lizzy. "Look around, Liz," he said. "Do you see anyone in this room who can play the banjo?"

"Well, no," she said with a shrug. "But we could learn, couldn't we?"

Scout Sister shook her head. "I hate to tell you this, Liz," she said, "but I haven't saved enough of my allowance to rent a banjo."

"Besides," said Scout Fred, "by the time we learned to play well enough to get the badge, the summer would be long gone."

"Yeah," said Brother. "And I've got better things to do than sittin' and strummin' day and night for the rest of the summer. Hey, Fred, crack that book and check out the list. There must be something easier. Or at least quicker."

A copy of the *Official Bear Scout Handbook* rested next to Fred's place on the top plank of the old chicken roost the scouts had turned into benches. He opened it and thumbed through to the list of merit badges. "Hmm," he said. "What about the Popsicle Stick Art Merit Badge?"

"What do we have to do to get it?" asked Brother.

Fred read the entry aloud. "'The scout troop must construct an original work of art made entirely from Popsicle sticks. An exact total of fifty thousand sticks must be used.'"

"Oh great," muttered Sister. "Sounds *hard.*"

"Come off it, Sis," said Lizzy. "It'd be easy. We could just glue all the sticks into a long, thin, flattened bunch."

"And what would that make?" asked Sister.

"A giant Popsicle stick!"

"A giant Popsicle stick made of Popsicle sticks?" said Fred with a smile.

"That's not art!" Brother snorted.

"Oh no?" said Lizzy. "You're forgetting the collage that Mr. Smock accepted from Too-Tall in art class last term."

"You mean the one where Too-Tall took a sledgehammer to a watermelon and a bunch of grapes and called it *Fruit*

Salad?" said Brother. "How could anyone forget that?"

"What *you* are forgetting, Lizzy," said Fred, "is that although Mr. Smock accepted the collage, he gave it a D minus.

And that would hardly be good enough to earn the Fruit Art Merit Badge. If there were such a thing."

"Besides," said Brother, "how would we get fifty thousand Popsicle sticks?"

Lizzy grinned sheepishly. "By eating fifty thousand Popsicles?"

"Good idea," said Brother. "That way we could go for the Stomachache Merit Badge at the same time."

"But there isn't any Stomachache Merit Badge," said Lizzy, frowning.

"No," said Brother. "But if the four of us ate fifty thousand Popsicles by the end of the summer, they'd have to create one in our honor."

"He's kidding," Sister whispered in Lizzy's ear. Lizzy had the sharpest hearing of any cub in Bear Country, but when what her ears heard was a joke, her brain didn't always get it.

"I give up," sighed Brother. "There's just

nothing interesting left on the list."

The scouts sat brooding, with glum looks on their faces. What they didn't know was that they were about to hear a rapping at the clubhouse window, a rapping that would set in motion a chain of events that would solve their problem.

"What's that noise?" said Sister.

"Sounds like a chicken pecking at the window," said Lizzy.

The sound came again. And for once Lizzy's sharp ears were mistaken.

"Hey, look," said Fred. "Look who it is!"

Farmer Ben stood at the window, sweating heavily in the hot summer sun.

"Why is Farmer Ben rapping on our window?" said Sister.

"He's too big to fit through the door," said Lizzy. The only way you could enter the clubhouse was through a hole in the old hollow tree stump that stood right up against the coop.

"I meant what does he want?" said Sister.

Farmer Ben was getting impatient. "Open up!" he yelled. "It's hot outside!"

Fred raised the window and said, "So now it's cold outside?"

"Very funny," said Ben, wiping his face with a handkerchief. He handed a piece of notepad paper to Fred. "Message from Scout Leader Jane."

"Message from Scout Leader Jane?" said Sister. "Hey, wait a minute, Farmer Ben. Did you tell her where our secret clubhouse is?"

"Absolutely not," said Ben.

"Then how come she knew to give *you* the message to deliver?" said Lizzy.

"Last week I sort of let it slip that I know where the clubhouse is," Ben admitted. "But I never said *where* it is. I'm tempted to, though. Don't want to become your messenger service."

"You *can't* tell, Ben!" said Brother. "You're the only one who knows, and it's gotta stay that way! Please, Ben, we'll make you Honorary Bear Scout Messenger!"

"I'll settle for Honorary Bear Scout Chump," said Ben. "Don't worry, scouts. Your secret is safe with me." He rested his elbows on the windowsill and leaned into the room. "Whew! It's as hot inside as it is outside!"

"No kidding," said Sister. "Why didn't you ever air-condition this place?"

"Maybe my brain is a bit fried by the sun today," said Ben, "but I can't imagine who in the world would want an air-conditioned chicken coop."

"A chicken with heatstroke?" suggested Brother.

"Very funny again," said Ben. "You scouts are a million laughs. Wish I could stay and laugh some more, but I'd better get out of this sun before I shrivel up like a prune."

As Farmer Ben trudged off across the field, the scouts gathered around Fred to read the message. It said: "Attention, Bear Scouts! Meet me at the office of Bruin, Bruin, Bruin, and Grizzly at 12th and Elm at three o'clock this afternoon." It was signed "Scout Leader Jane."

"Hmm," said Fred. "Those must be lawyers."

"What do you suppose it's about?" asked Sister.

"Three o'clock is only twenty minutes from now," said Brother, glancing at his watch. "We'd better hurry. We can do our supposing on the way."

• Chapter 3 •

Bruin, Bruin, Bruin, and Grizzly

The law offices of Bruin, Bruin, Bruin, and Grizzly were located in one of the most impressive buildings in downtown Beartown. It had four stories, and the offices were on the top floor. The scouts took the elevator up. The door opened directly onto a spacious waiting room. They saw BRUIN, BRUIN, BRUIN, AND GRIZZLY in big raised gold letters on the wall behind the receptionist's desk.

"Wow!" said Fred. "They've got a whole floor!"

"Yeah," said Sister. "And the walls and ceilings, too!"

Scout Leader Jane was already there. No sooner had the scouts taken seats beside her than the receptionist looked up and announced, "Lawyer Bruin will see you now."

They were shown into an office, where they sat in chairs in front of Lawyer Bruin's big desk. Jane seemed calm, but the scouts were nervous. What was it all about? Were they in trouble? Had they broken some law? Was Ralph Ripoff suing them for foiling one of his crooked schemes?

"Good afternoon," said Lawyer Bruin. "Tell me, have any of you ever heard of the Widow Bearkin?"

Jane and the scouts looked at each other. None of them spoke until Lizzy asked, "Is she related to the Widder Mc-Grizz?"

"No," said Lawyer Bruin. "The Widow Bearkin doesn't have any relations left in the Beartown area. Or *didn't* have any, I should say. She passed on last week at the age of ninety-seven."

"Passed on what?" asked Sister.

Brother leaned over to Sister and whispered, "He means she died."

"I have in front of me," continued Lawyer Bruin, "the Widow Bearkin's last will and testament. Let me read one section of it to you." He turned a few pages of the will and read: "'I hereby leave to the Beartown Bear Scout Troop the real property known as Spook Hill and all buildings, outbuildings, and other features thereon.'"

"*Thereon?*" said Sister.

Lawyer Bruin smiled. "It just means 'on it,'" he said. "It's lawyer talk. We write legal documents this way so folks will have to hire us to explain them."

Jane turned to the scouts. "Do you realize what this means?" she said.

"Sure," said Lizzy. "It means the mystery of who owns Spook Hill is solved. It's the Widow Bearkin."

"*Was* the Widow Bearkin," Jane corrected her. "Now *we're* the owners of Spook Hill."

WIDOW BEARKIN

Suddenly it dawned on the scouts. Their eyes grew wide.

"That means we own the *House* on Spook Hill!" said Fred.

"And the graveyard *beside* the House on Spook Hill!" added Brother.

"That's exactly right," said Lawyer Bruin. "You cubs have sharp legal minds."

"But why would anyone want the House on Spook Hill?" wondered Lizzy.

"Or the graveyard?" said Sister.

"They're both haunted!"

"Nonsense," said Jane. "That's just old-fashioned superstition." She turned to Lawyer Bruin. "I don't remember anyone ever living on Spook Hill. Did the Widow Bearkin?"

"Oh, no, she never lived on Spook Hill," said Lawyer Bruin. "She lived for many years all by herself in a little house out near Birder's Woods. The Spook Hill property was bought by the Bearkin family over two hundred years ago, and it's been handed down from one generation to the next ever since."

"Then why didn't the widow hand it down to the next Bearkin generation?" asked Jane.

"In a letter attached to her will," Lawyer Bruin explained, "she writes that many, many years ago some Bear Scouts of yore helped her cross Main Street when she was feeling dizzy on a hot summer day. She never forgot that kindness, and as a token of her appreciation she has left the Spook Hill property to the Beartown scout troop."

"But what are we supposed to do with it?" asked Brother. "And what are we supposed to do about the ghosts?"

"The answer to your first question is simple," said Lawyer Bruin. "You are to take possession of the property. As for your question about ghosts, that is no concern of mine. But there's more. The will goes on to stipulate —"

"That means 'say,'" Brother whispered to Sister.

"— that in order to disprove the claim that Spook Hill and structures thereon are haunted, and that you Bear Scouts are worthy of this gift, you must first prove that you have the gift of courage. You must take possession of the hill and the house thereon at twelve midnight, at the time of the next new moon."

Sister laughed. "That's crazy!" she said. "I wouldn't set foot inside that house at twelve *noon*!"

The other scouts murmured in agreement.

"That may be," said Lawyer Bruin. "Nevertheless, those are the Widow Bearkin's terms, and if you wish to inherit, you must follow them to the letter."

"What happens if we don't?" asked Brother.

"Then the property goes to the county to do with as it pleases," said Lawyer Bruin.

"Good!" said Brother.

"So be it!" said Sister.

"The county can have it!" said Fred.

"And do with it as it pleases!" added Lizzy.

Scout Leader Jane just sat patiently, saying not a word.

• Chapter 4 •

Pros and Cons

From the law offices of Bruin, Bruin, Bruin, and Grizzly the scouts went straight to Scout Leader Jane's house for milk and cookies. While they took care of their grumbling tummies, they discussed the pros and cons of accepting their inheritance.

"I don't even need to hear the pros," said Sister. "The cons are good enough for me."

"Like a haunted house," said Lizzy.

"And a haunted graveyard," said Fred.

"And don't forget a belfry full of scary bats," added Brother.

"Nonsense," said Jane. "That's just a bunch of old stories."

"And one *not-so-old* story," said Fred. "Remember when the Too-Tall Gang went up there last summer?"

"I don't believe their story for a minute," said Jane. "They probably made up the whole thing. Besides, I didn't realize any of you cubs believed in ghosts in the first place."

The scouts looked at each other a bit sheepishly.

"I don't," said Sister. "But I'm still afraid of them."

"Me, too," said Lizzy.

"Me, three," said Fred.

Brother looked more embarrassed than the others. "Me, four," he finally admitted. "But it's not just us cubs, Scout Leader Jane. Do you remember when several townsbears who live closest to Spook Hill complained to Chief Bruno about all the moaning and wailing?"

"Yes, I do," said Jane. "But those noises were never confirmed. Chief Bruno said it was the state police's job to check them out because Spook Hill is outside of Beartown township. The state police claimed just the opposite. So the complaints were never investigated. I think folks were just imagining things."

"Even imaginary ghosts are enough to

scare me," said Sister. "There's no way I'm going into that creepy old house at midnight. Not for love or money."

"But that's exactly why we *should* accept the inheritance," said Jane. "For love *and* money."

"Huh?" chorused the scouts.

"That's right," said Jane. "We should accept the Widow Bearkin's gift for love of the truth that there are no such things as ghosts and for the money that the place is worth."

"Money?" said Brother. "How much money?"

"Thousands and thousands of dollars," said Jane. "Why, the real estate alone would bring enough to keep our troop going for at least another century without a single fund-raiser. Besides, I just got a list of new business merit badges from Bear Scouts headquarters in Big Bear City, and it includes a Real Estate Merit Badge.

And while I can't make any promises, it seems to me that dealing with the House on Spook Hill could be worth a merit badge."

Despite their fears, the scouts began to warm to the idea of taking over Spook Hill and its haunted house. Apart from the merit badge, they talked about all the things they could buy with the money from the sale of the property — things like

a hot-air balloon, a motorboat, water skis, and all kinds of camping equipment, including the very best tents, lanterns, and sleeping bags. Or they could sell part of the land and keep the house for their own use. They could make the house into a super-duper scout headquarters that would make their old chicken coop clubhouse look like . . . well, a chicken coop.

"We still have time to check out the place before sundown," said Jane. "What do you say?"

The cubs looked at each other. "I d-d-d-dunno about that," said Sister with a shiver.

"We don't have to go inside the house yet, or even up the hill," Jane explained. "We can just look at it from the road. We don't even have to get out of the car."

That persuaded the scouts. They cleaned up their snack mess and piled into Jane's station wagon. And off they went.

• Chapter 5 •
Practice Run

Scout Leader Jane took the rutted road carefully, swerving to avoid cracks and potholes. It felt funny to be riding out of town in the "wrong" direction. The countryside was similar to the countryside along the road to Big Bear City — rolling hills, fields, forests — except for one thing. There were no houses, no malls, no auto graveyards — no sights that suggested the presence of bearkind.

Then, all of a sudden, the road ended.

"Hey, look over there!" said Lizzy, pointing. "There it is!"

Spook Hill loomed to their left. It was huge, much bigger than any of them had expected. It was overgrown with creepers and thorny under-brush.

"Hey," said Fred, "there's the narrow path Too-Tall talked about. It's really overgrown, just like he said."

Their gazes followed it up the hill, through the gate in the iron fence that surrounded the property, to the house. They could make out some broken win-dows and an ancient, crumbling belfry, but in the daylight the House on Spook Hill didn't look particularly scary. Just old and neglected.

"I think it's kind of cute," said Jane.

"'Cute' isn't the word that comes to mind," said Sister. "I'll bet it's full of ghosts, just like Too-Tall said. And the graveyard, too. If he was telling the truth about the overgrown path, then he was

probably telling the truth about every-
thing else."

Brother rolled his eyes. "That just
doesn't make sense, Sis," he said. "I'll bet
the moment the gang saw that overgrown
path they turned around and went home.
They probably cut up their fur with scis-
sors just to make their story look good."

"Good for you, Brother!" said Jane. "I'm

glad to see you've changed your tune. I had a feeling that bringing you out here in the daytime would help." She looked up the hill again. "I said this property could be worth thousands. Well, now that I see how big it is I admit I was wrong. It could be worth *millions*! We'd be nuts not to accept it as a gift!"

The scouts started adding all kinds of gadgets and gizmos to their list of future purchases. They weren't being guided by love and money anymore. They were being guided by love *of* money.

As soon as they got back to town, Fred checked his almanac and found that the next new moon was only two days away. Jane suggested the scouts have a sleepover at her house on the evening of the big takeover. They would catch a few hours of sleep before Jane woke them shortly before midnight. Then they'd be off to Spook Hill again.

• Chapter 6 •

A Dreary Ditty

"Pass the blackberries, please," said Grizzly Gran.

"Here you are, Gran," said Mama Bear.

It was the day of the big takeover. The Bear family had invited Gramps and Gran to dinner to celebrate the scouts' good fortune. The whole town was talking about it. The day before, the news had been in the *Beartown Gazette* and on the local TV station.

"Well, cubs," said Gran, "are you ready to take possession of Spook Hill?"

"You bet," said Brother. "And all buildings, outbuildings, and other features thereon."

Gramps frowned. "You been studyin' to become a lawyer, Brother?" he asked.

"It was in the Widow Bearkin's will," said Brother. "Did you know she owned Spook Hill, Gramps?"

"Yup," said Gramps. "Quite a few folks used to know it. Seems like the younger generation sort of forgot. Probably because no one lived there for so long."

"Did you know her?" asked Sister.

"Not personally," said Gramps. "I saw her once or twice in town years ago."

"She must have already been a grown-up when you were still a cub," said Brother. "She lived to be ninety-seven, you know."

"That's what most folks say," said Gramps.

"Most folks?" said Sister. "What do the rest say?"

"That she lived to be *sixty*-seven," said Gramps, "and only *looked* ninety-seven."

"Sixty-seven?" said Brother. "That's a difference of thirty years. How could that be?"

Gramps turned to Papa Bear. "Son, do you remember that little ditty cubs used to recite when you were a youngster?"

When Papa shook his head no, Gramps leaned back in his chair and looked around the table at everyone. He had that little twinkle in his eye that he got whenever he was about to say something he thought was especially clever. "Well, *I* remember it," he said. "It goes like this:

The Widow Bearkin drove through town
In her old convertible with the top down.
She drove up Spook Hill
When the moon was bright
And aged thirty years overnight.

"Hush up, Gramps!" snapped Gran. "You'll scare the cubs with talk like that!"

But it was too late. Sister's footsteps could already be heard thumping on the stairs. Then a bedroom door slammed.

"Now you've gone and done it, you old coot!" Gran scolded. "And on the very night the scouts have to take possession of the place!"

"What did I say?" Gramps protested. "It's just a silly old ditty. It's part of Beartown history. The cubs have always liked history in school. . . ."

"*Spook Hill* history is different," said Mama.

"Don't worry, Gramps," said Brother. "I'll go talk to Sister."

As Brother headed upstairs, Gramps turned to Papa and asked, "Are you sure it's safe for the cubs to go to Spook Hill in the middle of the night?"

"Oh, sure," said Papa. "Scout Leader Jane will be with them every minute."

"Well, in that case, there's nothin' to worry about," said Gramps. But as he spooned out a second helping of blackberries, he was heard to mutter, "*I hope.*"

Then the doorbell rang. It was Scout Leader Jane, right on time for the fateful pickup.

• Chapter 7 •
A Date with Destiny

"Wake up, scouts," said a voice. "It's time."

One by one the scouts opened their eyes to see Scout Leader Jane beaming down at them. She had to be as excited as they were. But she seemed calm and collected. The scouts, though sleepy, were very nervous. The butterflies in their stomachs were already starting to get restless. Especially the ones in Sister's stomach. Despite Brother's calming talk with her earlier, she couldn't help playing Gramps's little ditty over and over in her head.

The scouts were out of their sleeping bags before any of them noticed there was someone else in the room besides Scout Leader Jane.

"Lawyer Bruin!" said Brother. "What are you doing here?"

The lawyer smiled. He looked as calm and collected as Jane, and that made the scouts feel a little calmer, too. "My law firm has given me the task of accompanying you to Spook Hill as an observer," he said.

"Why?" asked Fred.

"To make sure that you fulfill the terms of the Widow Bearkin's will," said Lawyer Bruin. "You must enter the House on Spook Hill at midnight. In order to prove it isn't haunted, you must go into every room on each floor at least once, including the basement. And, finally, you must stay in the house until dawn."

"That's why we're taking our sleeping bags, scouts," said Jane.

"What about snacks?" asked Fred.

"I've already packed some," said Jane.

"Better take a lot," said Sister. " 'Cause I don't think we're gonna be doing a lot of sleeping."

The scouts stuffed their sleeping bags back into the sacks and tied them to their backpacks. Then they piled into Jane's station wagon and headed off, followed closely by Lawyer Bruin in his silver Bearcedes-Benz. They drove through a deserted downtown. All the familiar landmarks — Town Hall, Bear Country Hospital, Biff Bruin's Pharmacy, the Burger Bear — stood empty and silent in the glow of the streetlamps.

"I've never been out this late," said Fred. "It looks like a ghost town."

"Hey!" said Sister. "Try not to say 'ghost' anymore tonight!"

"Yeah!" said Lizzy. "Not while we're going to Spook Hill in the dead of night!"

"Cut it out, Liz!" whined Sister. "Don't say 'spook'! Or 'dead,' either!"

"Sorry," said Lizzy.

If it had felt funny riding out of town in the "wrong" direction in broad daylight, it felt much worse now. It felt absolutely, positively *weird*. The countryside was bathed in the dimmest of light from the sliver of new moon overhead. The forest looked like armies of many-armed monsters. Brother and Fred, realizing that the younger cubs were more frightened than they, did their best to calm them down. Once, when the headlights caught a bat flitting across the road, Brother put his hand on Sister's knee and said, "Don't worry, Sis. Bats can't hurt you."

"But what if they're *vampire* bats?" said Sister.

"No vampire bats around here," said Fred.

"How do you know that?" asked Lizzy.

"I read it in Professor Actual Factual's *Field Guide to Bear Country Mammals*, published by the Bearsonian Institution."

"*You've* read it," said Sister, "but have the *vampire bats* read it?"

"Of course not," said Fred. "Their eyesight is too poor."

That got a laugh from both Sister and Lizzy and helped them loosen up a little.

At last the two cars reached the end of the road. Spook Hill looked even bigger at night. The upper half of the house, with its crumbling belfry, was barely visible in the meager moonlight.

When the scout troop and its leader had gotten out of the car and put their backpacks back on, Jane looked over to where Lawyer Bruin had parked. "Are you coming?" she called.

"Er, uh . . . actually, no," came the lawyer's voice in the darkness. It sounded shaky and higher-pitched than it had at Jane's house. Jane shined her flashlight at his face. He didn't look the least bit calm anymore. In fact, he looked more nervous than Sister and Lizzy. "I've decided to observe from down here," he said. "You see . . . I, er, twisted my knee playing tennis yesterday, and that hike up the hill looks mighty rough."

The scouts looked at each other. "That's funny," said Sister. "He didn't say anything about his knee being sore back at Jane's house."

"And he wasn't limping, either," Fred pointed out.

Jane shushed them. "But how will you be sure that we enter every room?" she called.

"Er . . . I'll see your flashlights in the upstairs windows," said Lawyer Bruin. "That way at least I'll know you covered both floors."

"But what about the basement?" asked Brother.

"Oh . . . er, well . . . I'll take your word for it about the basement."

Fred leaned over to Jane and whispered, "Do you think we should get it in writing?"

"No, Fred," said Jane. "He's not trying to trick us out of our inheritance. He's just a little . . . well, scared. Maybe he believes in gh ——, er, I mean *you-know-whats.*"

"Even if he doesn't believe in you-know-whats," said Sister, "I can understand why he might not want to go up You-Know-What Hill in the you-know-what of night."

Jane looked up the hill. "Well, scouts," she said, "we need to get up there by midnight." She shined her flashlight at her wristwatch. "We'd better get going. Flashlights all on, scouts?"

"Check!" barked each scout in turn.

"Then I think this is the perfect time for our slogan," said Jane.

Jane and the scouts crossed their lit flashlights and shouted, "One for all and all for one!"

And up Spook Hill they went.

• Chapter 8 •

Spooked on Spook Hill

The tangle of creepers and thornbushes on the overgrown path had looked pretty nasty from the road, but it was much worse to hike through than it looked. The scouts had to keep pulling hats out of thornbushes and thorns out of hats. Once, Brother had a tug-of-war with a huge thornbush that seemed to want his sleeping bag in the worst way. By the time they reached the top of the hill, their pants were so covered with burs that they seemed to be wearing fuzzy leggings. After picking the thorns and burs out of their clothing, Jane and the scouts looked around, shining their flashlights in all directions.

"There's the graveyard, off to the left," said Jane.

"See any y-y-y-you-know-whats?" asked Sister, trembling.

"Absolutely none," said Jane firmly.

"You mean not yet," muttered Sister to herself.

Pretty soon the five flashlight beams came together on the house. "Oh, my goodness," said Lizzy in a hushed voice. "That's the *spookiest* house I ever saw."

Brother and Fred weren't as scared as the two younger cubs. But the house that had looked just old and neglected in the daytime and from a distance looked spooky enough now to make their hearts beat faster. The broken windows resembled gaping mouths with sharp, jagged teeth. And the moment the flashlight

beams fell on the crumbling old belfry above, it spat out a stream of bats.

"YIIIEEE!" screamed the scouts all at once.

When they'd gotten their breaths back, Brother put his arm around Sister's shoulders and said, "Remember, Sis, these bats can't h-h-hurt you. Just insect eaters. Like the ones in Giant Bat Cave."

"Hey," said Fred, aiming his flashlight up the steps of the front porch. "It looks like somebody wrote something on the door."

Slowly, Jane and the scouts made their way up the creaky steps to the porch. Scratched into the splintery old wood of the front door were four names: Too-Tall, Skuzz, Smirk, and Vinnie.

"So they *did* come up here, after all," said Fred. "They weren't lying about the burs in their fur."

Brother noticed Sister looking nervously over at the graveyard. "Now, Sis," he said, "that *doesn't* mean they told the truth about the gh ——, er, those other

things."

"Well said, Brother," said Jane. "Because burs are real, and we all know there are no such things as those other things." She glanced at her watch again. "Twelve o'clock sharp. It's now or never, scouts. . . ." She grasped the big brass doorknob.

"Wait!" said Sister. "We've got to go back to Jane's! I forgot something!"

"What did you forget, Sis?" asked Brother.

"I forgot to *stay there*!" wailed Sister.

"There's no turning back now!" said Jane. "Be brave, scouts!" She turned the knob and pushed.

The door swung open. *C-r-r-e-e-a-a-k-k*. Jane led the way into a high-ceilinged room. It might have been the living room, but it was kind of hard to imagine anyone living in it. The stink of mildew attacked the scouts' nostrils. They shined their flashlights over a lot of old dusty furniture that appeared to be knitted all together with cobwebs.

"Sort of like a connect-the-dots picture, with the furniture as dots," said Fred. "Heh-heh."

But Fred's attempt at humor fell on deaf ears.

Suddenly Sister said, "What's that?" She pointed across the room.

The others turned to see as many as half a dozen pairs of little yellow eyes glaring at them from the floor near the far wall. The eyes flared as the flashlight beams found them.

"Rats!" cried Lizzy.

"YIIIEEE!" screamed the scouts all together. Sister's scream lasted the longest. As her voice trailed off, it was replaced by another's rising.

"WHO-O-O-O-O!"

Everyone froze. The haunting wail

seemed to have come from upstairs. If they'd been in a jollier mood, one of the scouts might have cracked a joke about Sister being a great ventriloquist. But jokes were the furthest thing from their minds.

"W-W-What was that?" said Fred.

Another "WHO-O-O-O-O!"

"There it is again!" said Lizzy. "It's not an owl." Lizzy could recognize animal sounds as well as anyone in Bear Country. If she said it wasn't an owl, it wasn't.

Still another "WHO-O-O-O-O!"

"It's a . . . a . . . a *you-know-what!*" shrieked Sister. "I'm outta here!"

But as Sister turned to run, Brother grabbed her arm. "Wait, Sis! There's something odd about all this. Those rats are completely still!"

"And that wail is exactly the same every time," said Jane. "I'm going upstairs to check it out. Who's coming with me?"

• Chapter 9 •

Do Drop In

All four scouts followed Jane upstairs, not because they had any desire to check out the ghostly wail but because they were terrified of being left behind. Inching their way up the long dark stairway wasn't exactly the most fun they had ever had. Halfway up they found their path blocked by a huge cobweb with a big black spider in its center. The ugly creature was so big that it looked like a hairy black hand with long curved fingers. Scout Leader Jane bravely used her flashlight as a club to knock away the web and its terrifying

weaver. Meanwhile, the ghostly wail came closer and closer as they climbed. "WHO-O-O-O-O!"

Finally, they reached the top of the stairs and followed the sound to a closed door. Jane took hold of the doorknob. "Ready, scouts?" she said. "Here goes . . ."

Jane flung open the door, and they all shined their flashlights into the room. What they saw made their knees knock together.

"It's a g-g-*ghost*!" shrieked Sister.

They all screamed at the top of their lungs.

All except Jane, that is. In an instant she was face-to-face with the bear-sized white figure, her flashlight raised again like a club. She struck the ghost a single blow, and it crumpled to the floor, where it lay in a motionless heap. "It's just a sheet," said Jane, "hung from the ceiling by a string!"

But the wail kept wailing. Maybe it was the ghost of the ghost!

But Jane wasn't fooled. She was already inspecting a bed that had been concealed from view by the sheet. It was an old-fashioned four-poster with a lace canopy. And it was quite a sight. Cobwebs wound about the bedposts and over the canopy. In fact, it wasn't easy to tell how much of the canopy was lace and how much of it was cobwebs.

"Aha!" said Jane. "Just as I thought! *Here's* our ghost!"

The scouts hurried to Jane's side. There, sitting in the middle of the bed, was a boom box. As the scouts stared, it spoke: "WHO-O-O-O!"

"It's a recording!" cried Brother. "The ghost that just made us scream our heads off is just a *recording*!"

"You know what this means, scouts?" said Jane.

"Yeah!" said Brother. "It means someone is trying to scare us away from this
house!"

"And probably away from Spook Hill al-
together!" added Fred.

"To keep us from taking possession of
our inheritance?" asked Sister.

"Exactly," said Jane.

"But why?" asked Lizzy.

"That I don't know," said Jane. "What I
know is that we should go straight to the
police station and report this to Chief
Bruno."

"Wait a minute," said Sister. "What
about the terms of the will?"

"What about them?" said Brother.

"We have to stay here all night," said Sister. "And we haven't been in the basement yet."

"Forget about the basement, Sis," said Brother. "Lawyer Bruin said he'd take our word for it about the basement."

"But that's dishonest," said Sister. "In the Bear Scout Oath it says, 'A Bear Scout is as honest as the day is long.'"

"Well, this is the middle of the night," said Fred. "Besides, the bad guys who are trying to scare us might be hiding in the basement!"

"Yikes!" said Sister. "Let's get outta here!"

But the House on Spook Hill had other ideas. Before the scouts could get moving, they felt a trembling beneath their feet and heard a long, drawn-out *c-r-r-e-e-a-a-k-k*!

"What was that?" said Lizzy.

"Felt like an earthquake!" said Fred.

But it wasn't an earthquake. It was the old rotting floorboards about to give way.

And then they did give way. *CRASH!*

The group managed one more scream: "YIIIEEE!"

Scout Leader Jane, the Bear Scouts, and the four-poster all went crashing through the floor into the living room. But they didn't stop there. Because the old rotting *living room* floorboards gave way, too.

Down they fell into the basement below. Luckily, they were saved by the big old bed, which landed first. Jane and the scouts came crashing through the lace canopy, right onto the thick mattress.

For a moment they lay dazed, a tangle of arms, legs, backpacks, and cobwebs. Brother, Sister, and Lizzy all had lost their flashlights. Jane and Fred shined theirs around the room.

"Nobody here but us scouts," announced Jane.

All at once the scouts let out huge sighs

of relief. "Whew!" said Brother. "That was close!"

"At least we *did* get to the basement," said Sister.

Suddenly, there was another tremor beneath them, followed by a low shuddering sound.

"Uh-oh," said Sister. "What was that?"

"It's the floor!" said Fred. "It's straining under our weight!"

"But it's solid concrete!" cried Brother.

"And it's a *basement* floor!" said Jane. "There's nothing under it but solid earth!"

But the House on Spook Hill had one more surprise in store for the Bear Scouts. The *basement* floor gave way!

Down they went again — Jane, scouts, and all — into . . .

Total darkness.

• Chapter 10 •

Spook Hill Surprise

This time the big four-poster shattered into several dozen pieces when it hit bottom. Jane and the scouts were thrown to the floor — or, rather, to the *ground*. They could feel the cold earth beneath them. Luckily, they had all landed on their backs.

"Wow!" breathed Sister. "Saved by a sleeping bag!"

"Me, too!" came the voices of the other scouts, each in turn.

"Thank goodness you're all okay!" said

Jane. "Does anyone have a flashlight? I lost mine."

There was a clicking sound, followed by Fred saying, "Darn! Mine's broken!"

"Oh, no!" moaned Sister. "What are we gonna do?" She gazed up into the darkness above. Was that the outline of a big hole in the ceiling where they had come crashing through? She could barely make it out, so weak was the light from the new moon shining through the windows two and three floors above.

Just then a much brighter light shone down at them from the hole in the ceiling. "Hello?" said a voice. "Are you scouts down there?"

"That sounds like Lawyer Bruin," said Brother. "He must have heard all the crashing."

"Yes!" called Jane. "We're down here! And we're all right!"

"Hold on!" said the lawyer. "I'll look for a way down!" The light disappeared. "There's a trapdoor over here!"

Moments later, the light reappeared at the scouts' level. "A secret stairway!" said Lawyer Bruin. "Into a secret underground chamber! My goodness! It's like a cave! And it's full of cardboard boxes!"

Jane asked him to find their missing flashlights, and he wandered around among the boxes and the debris from the smashed bed until he found all three. Only Jane's and Brother's were still working.

"Aha!" said Jane as soon as she switched on her recovered flashlight. "Look at *this* box!"

Lawyer Bruin, Brother, Sister, and Lizzy made their way over to Jane. She had landed right next to a box on which was printed *Beartown Theatrical Supply: rubber rats with glow-in-the-dark eyes.*

"So *that's* why the rats didn't move,"

said Sister. "They're just as phony as that boom-box ghost."

Jane shifted the light to an empty plastic package beside the box. Across the top of it was a cardboard strip that read

BEARTOWN THEATRICAL SUPPLY— GIANT RUBBER SPIDER WITH SPIDER WEB

BEARTOWN THEATRICAL SUPPLY RUBBER RATS WITH GLOW-IN-THE-DARK EYES

Beartown Theatrical Supply: giant rubber spider with spiderweb.

"And that's why I was brave enough to club it with my flashlight," Jane admitted. "I suspected it was fake. Hey, where's Fred?"

"Right over here," said Fred. "I'm gonna open one of these bigger boxes." The others crowded around Fred as he cut open a box with his Bear Scout knife. "Holy smokes!" he cried. "A computer!"

"A computer?" said Sister. "What's a computer doing in a cave?"

Fred was already cutting open a second box. "Another one!" he said. "And they both look brand-new. What's going on here?"

The other scouts got out their Bear Scout knives and helped Fred open a whole bunch of boxes. Not only were there more computers in them, there were printers, TV sets, and lots of video-game players.

"*I'll* tell you what's going on here," said Lawyer Bruin. "Illegal activity. And you don't need to be a lawyer to see that!"

"Someone's using this secret room to store stolen loot," said Jane. "And electronics equipment seems to be their specialty."

"That must be why they tried to scare us away," said Brother. "To keep us from finding out about their crooked operation."

"But how in the world would they get this stuff out of here?" asked Fred.

"Easy," said Lizzy. "Up the secret stairway and the basement stairs, out the front door, and down Spook Hill."

"You call that *easy*?" Sister laughed. "There's gotta be a better way."

After a little exploring, the scouts found the opening of a tunnel. "Here's the better way," said Jane. "This must lead underground to an exit somewhere beyond Spook Hill."

"Cool!" said Fred. "Let's check it out!"

"Let's not and say we did!" said Sister.

"I'm afraid Sister's right this time," said Jane. "The crooks could be hiding in that tunnel."

Just the thought of the crooks made the scouts scramble up the secret stairway in search of some fresh night air. As they dashed out the front door of the House on Spook Hill, Lawyer Bruin cried, "I'll lead the way down! I'm still covered with burs from the climb up, anyway!"

"Are you sure you can make it down with your bad knee?" asked Sister, winking at the others.

"Oh . . . er, sure," said the lawyer. "Funny thing . . . it was feeling a lot better by the time I heard all that crashing coming from the house."

"You must be a very fast healer," said Fred.

• Chapter 11 •

The Vanishing Loot

It was nearly two o'clock in the morning
when Lawyer Bruin, Jane, and the Bear
Scouts returned to Spook Hill with Chief
Bruno, Officer Marguerite, and a group of
citizens deputized by the chief. They
climbed Spook Hill and made their way
down into the dungeonlike room below the
basement. To the surprise of all, their
flashlights revealed a nearly empty chamber.

"Well," said Chief Bruno, "it looks like
the crooks got all the loot out before we
got here. I'd say you scouts had a very

close call. Obviously, those crooks were watching you the whole time. They could just as well have shipped you off with the loot." He drew his gun. "In fact, they might still be here."

At that very moment, someone stepped into the room from the tunnel.

"It's a crook!" shrieked Sister. "And *he's* got a gun, too!"

The other scouts would have screamed, but they were too tired. Besides, they could see that although Sister was right about the gun, she was wrong about the crook. In fact, he wasn't even close to being a crook. He was a state trooper.

"Trooper Jones!" said Chief Bruno. "What're *you* doing here?"

"Just thought I ought to check to see if the scouts were still here before questioning those crooks," said the trooper. He looked up at the hole in the ceiling. "Wow! Looks like you cubs had a bit of a fall!"

"But how did you know we'd be here?" asked Brother.

"We've been watching the Big Bear City end of this operation for several days," explained Trooper Jones. "We wiretapped their phone and finally got some info about the Beartown end of it just last night. They said something about Bear Scouts taking possession of Spook Hill at midnight tonight, the same time they had a big pickup scheduled. They didn't want to postpone the pickup, so they decided to scare you scouts away, then get the loot. Luckily, they even mentioned the tunnel and where it exits. So we let them load their trucks and nabbed 'em. My boys are holding them for questioning out there right now."

Brother, Fred, Lizzy, and even Jane just stood there with their mouths open. But Sister was turning a fiery red. "Do you mean you knew those creeps were gonna scare the wits out of us and you didn't warn us?" she cried.

Trooper Jones shrugged. "Sorry, scouts," he said. "Warning you could have messed up our whole plan. If you scouts hadn't shown up here tonight, the crooks might have gotten suspicious and dropped this place like a hot potato. You weren't in any real danger. There's no way we would have let the crooks hurt you in any way."

Sister was still furious. "I can't believe you did that to us!" she sputtered. "We screamed our heads off up there!"

"Tell you what," said Trooper Jones. "To make it up to you, I'll let you come along and watch while we make the arrest. Would you like that?"

Sister's mouth fell open to match the others'. "Cool!" they chorused.

Trooper Jones looked Lawyer Bruin up and down. "How come you don't have your Scout Leader uniform on?" he asked.

"Oh, Jane here is Scout Leader," said Lawyer Bruin. "I'm not even in the scout program. I'm a lawyer."

"A *lawyer*?" said the trooper, nearly choking on the word. "I'm not sure we want the likes of *you* coming along —"

"Please let him come," pleaded Sister. "He helped us when we were in big trouble."

"All right," said Trooper Jones to the lawyer. "But don't go handing out any business cards to crooks while we're trying to make an arrest. Promise?"

Lawyer Bruin raised his right hand in a Bear Scout salute. "Scout's honor!" he said. Then he gave a sheepish grin. "Or . . . lawyer's honor?"

"No comment," said Trooper Jones. "All right, everybody. Let's go! Follow me!"

• Chapter 12 •

Moving Night

The crowd followed Trooper Jones through the dank, dark tunnel as he barked orders into a walkie-talkie. After a few minutes' walk, they emerged from the exit, which was set in a hillside next to a highway. Out on the road, a line of three huge moving trucks stood surrounded by squad cars and a police van.

"Hey, *this* isn't the road to Big Bear City," said Lizzy.

"Not the Beartown one," said Jane. "It's Highway One. It merges with the Bear-

town road halfway between Beartown and Big Bear City."

"By using this highway," explained Trooper Jones, "the crooks avoided going through Beartown, where they might have been seen, even in the middle of the night. They would have looked pretty suspicious, wouldn't they? Three big trucks coming into town by way of a dead-end road?"

The scouts and deputies followed Trooper Jones to the lead truck and gathered around as he fired a question at the driver. "Whatcha got in these trucks, pal?"

The driver looked sullenly down at the trooper. "Household furnishings," he said. "We're movin' some folks to a new home."

Trooper Jones ordered his fellow troopers to open the trucks and examine their cargo. When this had been done, one of the troopers came over to Jones and said, "Must be a pretty strange home, sir. A home furnished entirely with computers, TVs, and video-game players."

"Okay!" barked Trooper Jones at the drivers and their passengers. "You're all under arrest!"

• Chapter 13 •

The End of History?

It turned out that the Spook Hill crooks belonged to the infamous Bogg Brothers Gang, that bunch of career criminals who lived out in Forbidden Bog. They were taken in the troopers' van directly to Bear Country Prison in Big Bear City. Chief Bruno didn't bother to argue with the state troopers about whether the crime had been committed mostly within Beartown township or outside it. He knew that Beartown's jail wasn't big enough to hold more than a few of the crooks anyway.

At first, Jane and the scouts were worried that Bruin, Bruin, Bruin, and Grizzly might try to back out of the inheritance deal because not all the terms of the will had been met. But Lawyer Bruin convinced his firm that the terms of the will *had* been met, after all — at least, in spirit. The purpose of requiring the scouts to enter every room of the House on Spook Hill and stay there overnight was to prove that the house wasn't haunted. According to Lawyer Bruin's reasoning, the scouts had proved that very thing — just by different means. For they had clearly uncovered the Bogg Brothers Gang's criminal operation in the House on Spook Hill. And that was more than enough proof that the house wasn't haunted. If it *had* been haunted, argued Lawyer Bruin, the crooks would never have used it as their storage depot. Not only did the other lawyers of Bruin, Bruin, Bruin, and Grizzly agree with this reasoning, they even got the town council to pass a special law ensuring that the transfer of property to the Bear Scouts was legal.

And what happened to Spook Hill and the old house thereon? Did the Bear Scouts sell them and make lots and lots of money? Interestingly enough, the answer is no. Although they received many good offers from real estate companies, the scouts decided instead to turn the House on Spook Hill into a community center for young and old. Spook Hill itself was made into a park and playground. Squire Grizzly, the richest bear in Bear Country, was so impressed with the scouts' generosity

that he funded the whole makeover. And
the town council saw to it that funds were
provided to the Highway Department for
repairing the old crumbling road out to
Spook Hill. Last but not least, the scouts
earned their Real Estate Merit Badge and

tacked it to the ribbon on the Honor Wall of their chicken coop clubhouse.

It wasn't as if the darker side of Spook Hill's history was simply forgotten, though. Sister Bear came up with a wonderful idea that created a new Beartown tradition. Every Halloween the Spook Hill Community Center became the House on Spook Hill all over again, as the Bear Scouts decked it out in rubber cobwebs, rubber rats with glow-in-the-dark eyes, and wailing, white-sheeted ghost-scouts who jumped out at visitors from behind curtains and doors. Since it had been proven beyond a shadow of a doubt that the old house wasn't *really* haunted, every year folks all over Bear Country could hardly wait to go there and scream their heads off — for fun.

And that, friends, is the story of how Spook Hill history finally came to an end. Well, that's not exactly true. Actually, new

chapters in the history of Spook Hill are being written to this day, every year, and all the year round. It's just that they aren't spooky anymore.

Except, that is, at Halloween . . .
"WHO-O-O-O-O!"

• About the Author •

Stan and Jan Berenstain have been writing and illustrating books about bears for more than thirty years. Their very first book about the Bear Scout characters was published in 1967. Through the years the Bear Scouts have done their best to defend the weak, catch the crooked, joust again the unjust, and rally against rottenness of all kinds. In fact, the scouts have done such a great job of living up to the Bear Scout Oath, the authors say, that "they deserve a series of their own."

Stan and Jan Berenstain live in Bucks County, Pennsylvania. They have two sons, Michael and Leo, and four grandchildren. Michael is an artist, and Leo is a writer. Michael did the pictures in this book.

Don't Miss

THE *Berenstain*
BEAR
SCOUTS

**and the
Evil Eye**

Ralph began to swing his watch in front of the arch-weasel. "Observe my watch," said Ralph in a low, spooky voice that he remembered from his carnival days. "Gently swinging . . . back and forth . . . gently swinging . . ."

But McGreed wasn't watching the watch. He was looking into Ralph's eyes.

"Your eyes are getting . . . heavy," said Ralph.

But it wasn't McGreed's eyes that were getting heavy.

"You feel . . . you feel a great need to

sleep," said Ralph, his voice getting weaker and his eyes beginning to close.

McGreed reached out and gently took the watch from Ralph's hand. "Do you hear me, Ralph?" he said. "Do you hear me?"

Ralph nodded his head.

"When you wake up," said McGreed, "you are no longer going to be Ralph. You are going to be Big Red Rooster, king of the barnyard, and it is your job to tell the world the sun has just come up." Then McGreed snapped his fingers and said, "Wake up, Big Red Rooster."

The effect was astounding. As soon as Ralph opened his eyes he began leaping around, flapping his arms, and screaming *"COCK-A-DOODLE-DOO! COCK-A-DOO-DLE-DOO!"*

"Amazing," said Stye.

"Astonishing," said Dr. Boffins.

McGreed let Ralph be Big Red Rooster

for a while. Then he said, "When I snap my fingers, you will once again be Ralph." He snapped his fingers and Ralph came to.

"Wha-what happened?" said Ralph, looking puzzled.

"Nothing to worry about," said McGreed with a grin. "You and I just had an evil eye contest, and I won. Now, let's get on with Operation Revenge!"